This is the story of

ARIEL
AND THE
SECRET
GROTTO

You can read along
with me in your book.
You will know it is time
to turn the page when
you hear the chimes
ring like this…

Let's begin now:

Narrator Roy Dotrice	**Girl** Katie Jane Johnston	**Engineered by** Jeff Sheridan at AudioVisions
Ariel Jodi Benson	**Boy** Adam Ryen	**Cover Art by** Rick Brown
Flounder Daniel Wilson	**Written by** Paula Sigman	**Inside Art by** Al White Studio
Sebastian Samuel E. Wright	**Produced by** Randy Thornton and Ted Kryczko	**Art Direction by** Paul Wenzel and James DiMauro
Scuttle Buddy Hackett		

Disney

ARIEL AND THE SECRET GROTTO

Includes the song "Part of Your World"!

Once, in the days when the mermaid princess Ariel was still young, and she knew the sun only as a glowing flower glimpsed far away through the vast blue sea, her best friend Flounder swam to her palace garden. "Pssst, Ariel. I found something I think you ought to see!"

"Why, what is it, Flounder?"

The little fish twirled with excitement. "That's just it! I don't know! I've never seen anything like it before."

Ariel followed the curious fish. Far away from the palace, a dark shape rose before them. "Oh, Flounder! It's a sunken ship! I've always wanted to explore one." She swam to a porthole and peered in. Something silvery glittered back at her. "I'm going in!" Ariel squeezed through the open porthole. Inside she found a treasure trove of artifacts from the human world! There were clocks and candlesticks, paintings and mirrors, even a china figure that danced when Ariel turned the key.

The little mermaid darted from treasure to treasure. "Isn't this wonderful? What do you suppose it's for?"

Flounder flipped his fins as she held up a fish hook. "Gee, Ariel, that looks sharp! Uh, maybe, we shouldn't be in here."

"What a scaredy-fish! There's nothing to worry about."

Suddenly a porthole swung open. "Ariel! I have been looking everywhere! How can you learn to sing if you are always missing your lessons?!" It was Sebastian, the Royal Court Composer.

"I'm sorry, Sebastian. But look! Isn't this place fantastic?"

The tiny crab shook his claw in disapproval. "You shouldn't be in here, child. Ships like dese, from de human world, dey are not'ing but trouble!"

"But Sebastian, how can something so beautiful be bad?"

He hopped onto a seachest. "Humans use dese ships to sail across de sea." He pointed to the fish hook. "And dey use dese to catch fish! Humans are barbarians!"

4

"You sound just like my father." Ariel whirled away and put on a beaded necklace, smiling at her reflection in the mirror.

"Humans are dangerous! Dat is why King Triton forbids contact with de human world. And dat includes dese human t'ings!"

Flounder came to Ariel's defense. "Aw, Sebastian. We were just looking."

"Don't tell me. Looking leads to wanting. And dat leads to trouble!" 5

Ariel held up a shiny candlestick. "But it must be such a wonderful world—to create such wonderful things. If only I were fifteen! I'd go up to the surface and see for myself."

"Dat is nonsense, Ariel. You know dat even if you were old enough, you can only go up dere once, on your fifteenth birthday. Don't even t'ink such a thought. I'm your teacher. If your father heard you talking like dat, I'd be one cracked crab!" Sebastian shooed Ariel and Flounder away from the ship. But as she left, Ariel snatched up a jewelled hairpin and hid it in her hands.

When Ariel returned to her room, she turned the hairpin over and over. The jewels sent a rainbow of colored lights dancing across the castle walls. "I don't see how anyone who makes such beautiful things can be all bad."

So in spite of her father's rule, Ariel was determined to learn more about the human world.

In the days and weeks that followed, Ariel and Flounder returned again and again to the ship. "Ariel, are you sure this is a good idea? Remember what Sebastian said."

"Oh, Flounder. He's just a worryfish." She picked up a soup bowl and studied it. "Look at this—this thingamabob! Why, I'll bet humans wear it on their heads!"

Flounder laughed. "What a funny-looking crown that makes!"

Flounder grew bolder. He explored every nook and cranny of the sunken ship, from the crow's nest at the top of its mast to the very bottom of its hull. "This is cool!"

Ariel opened a chest. It was full of gold coins. "These are pretty!" Ariel was delighted by her discovery.

Each time Ariel and Flounder visited the ship, Ariel brought one of the treasures out with her. "Don't worry, Flounder. No one will find out. Follow me."

Ariel led the little fish to a secret grotto, tucked away between a reef and a sea mountain. "This place is perfect. I can keep everything here, and no one will ever know. Just you and me."

Before long, Flounder and Ariel discovered another shipwreck, and soon they filled the grotto with more curios and oddities from the human world. "Isn't this a fabulous collection? Wish I knew what everything was for."

The undersea cavern became Ariel's secret retreat, where she wondered and thought and dreamed about what life was like up near the sun.

One day, Ariel and Flounder were playing with the treasures in the grotto. Ariel put on a pearl necklace and spun around, pretending to dance. Then all of a sudden she gasped. "Oh no! I'm going to be late for my music lesson again!" Ariel and Flounder pushed the huge rock that hid the entrance to the grotto into place and swam off.

Back at the palace, Sebastian eyed the little mermaid curiously. "Dere's somet'ing different about you dese days, Ariel."

"You must be imagining things, Sebastian. Listen to my scales!"

Sebastian pointed accusingly. "Where did you get dat necklace? Dose don't look like any mer-pearls I've seen!"

Ariel smiled. "Oh, these! Uh…."

Flounder chimed in. "I found them. I think they look pretty on Ariel. Anyway, all pearls come from the ocean, don't they?"

Sebastian frowned, but continued with Ariel's lesson.

Ariel whispered to Flounder. "Whew! That was a close one."

Later that afternoon, down in the sunken ship, Ariel and Flounder discovered a chamber they hadn't seen before. "B-be careful, Ariel. That looks dark and creepy!" But Ariel wasn't afraid. She kicked her tail and swam in.

Suddenly, the water surged up! A huge tentacle shot out of the blackness and wrapped itself around her. It was a giant octopus! The powerful arm squeezed the little mermaid and began pulling her deeper into the dark chamber. Ariel twisted in its grasp. "Let me go!" But the octopus only squeezed tighter.

Flounder darted back and forth, but there was nothing he could do. "Ariel!" The little mermaid wriggled and managed to free her hands. Then she pushed against the tentacles with all her might and gave a mighty kick. She suddenly broke free!

Ariel and Flounder swam away as fast as their tails could move them. "I'd better be more careful next time!"

15

A few days later, Flounder found Ariel dreaming in her grotto. "Flounder, I've decided. I'm not going to wait until my fifteenth birthday. I'm going up to the surface today!"

"But Ariel! You can't! It's not allowed!"

"I don't care. I'm going. I have to see what it's like." She swam resolutely to the grotto entrance. "You don't have to come."

Flounder swam after her in alarm. "Ariel! It's too dangerous! Come back, please!"

But it was no use. She sped upward from the ocean bottom, all the way to the bright turquoise water just below the waves.

The sun had nearly set when Ariel and Flounder broke the surface of the water. The clouds were rosy-pink, and along the horizon a band of gold sparkled and danced upon the sea. "Oh! Oh, Flounder! I never dreamed it would be so beautiful!"

Suddenly a flock of gulls wheeled towards them, spiraling and darting through the sky. One of them winked as he went by, but Flounder quickly dove under the water and then came back up. "Wow. What were those?"

"I don't know! Maybe fish that can fly?"

17

"Look, Flounder! Over there! Is that land?" Ariel dove and swam just under the surface, towards the shore. When they were still a good distance away, she bobbed to the surface again. "Oh my gosh! It's a little boat!"

As she watched, the boat came closer. She would be seen! She ducked back under the water and swam away, but just a little bit. This was her chance to find out more about the human world, and 18 she wasn't going to lose it.

A small boy and girl sat in the tiny rowboat, trailing their fingers in the water. Ariel looked up at them from beneath the waves. She was so close! Suddenly there was a splash! "Oh no! My dolly! I dropped it!"

Ariel dove after the doll as it sank through the water. She caught it and hugged it to her. "So this is what humans look like!" She spun away from the boat in joy and didn't even notice that the boy had dropped a fishing net into the water.

19

Ariel swam far below the boat, clutching the doll. She was safely out of sight, even if the children looked down into the water. The little girl was still upset. "I've lost my doll!"

The boy reached over the side of the boat. "Never mind that! I caught something!"

Below the water's surface, Flounder was struggling. "Ariel! Ariel, help!" Flounder was caught in the net! Ariel didn't know what to do. The boy hauled up the net and the boat began to move away.

Ariel let go of the doll and hurtled up toward the boat. But as she drew closer, the boy leaned over the side. "Aw, this is just a little guy." He gently slipped Flounder into the water. "Back you go, fella."

Flounder wiggled his fins faster than ever and swam back to Ariel. His eyes were as big as sand dollars. "Did you see that!"

"Oh, Flounder, I was so worried." Ariel hugged her friend.

21

Ariel watched the little boat floating away. She thought about how kind the humans had been to set Flounder free. Suddenly she streaked down through the water, snatched up the doll, and bobbed up to the surface again. "I wish I could keep this, but they were so nice. I ought to give it back. But how? I can't let them see me."

"Need help, sweetie?" It was the gull that had winked at her! "I can fix it for ya!" He took the doll in his beak, flew over to the boat, and dropped it into the arms of the little girl.

Just then Sebastian popped to the surface. "Ariel! Dere you are! What are you doin' up here, young lady? Oh, your father is gonna bust his scales when he finds out about dis. Dis is terrible! What if a human saw you? You'd wind up on a hook for sure! You two come home with me dis minute!"

Ariel took one last look at the sky, filling her heart with its beauty. "All right, Sebastian. We'll come home now." Then, just before they dove under the sea, she winked at Flounder. "But I'll be back."

The little mermaid promised herself this was just the beginning. Ariel knew Sebastian and her father must be wrong about the humans. She had seen for herself how kind they could be. She 24 hoped someday, somehow, she would be part of their world.